To my wonderful mum and dad,
with thanks to L and L xx
L.F.

For Liam, Lorna, Seb and Astrid
K.H.

First published 2023 by Nosy Crow Ltd, Wheat Wharf, 27a Shad Thames, London, SE1 2XZ, UK · Nosy Crow Eireann Ltd, 44 Orchard Grove, Kenmare, Co Kerry, V93 FY22, Ireland · www.nosycrow.com · ISBN 978 1 83994 679 0 (HB) · ISBN 978 1 83994 680 6 (PB) · Nosy Crow and associated logos are trademarks and/or registered trademarks of Nosy Crow Ltd. · Text © Louise Fitzgerald 2023 · Illustrations © Kate Hindley 2023 · The right of Louise Fitzgerald to be identified as the author and Kate Hindley to be identified as the illustrator of this work has been asserted. A CIP catalogue record for this book is available from the British Library. · Papers used by Nosy Crow are made from wood grown in sustainable forests. Printed and bound in China · 10 9 8 7 6 5 4 3 2 1 (HB) · 10 9 8 7 6 5 4 3 2 1 (PB)

THE QUICKEST BEDTIME STORY EVER!

THE QUICKEST BEDTIME STORY EVER!

LOUISE FITZGERALD & KATE HINDLEY

nosy crow

Great news! This book contains the quickest bedtime story EVER!

It's a **brilliant** story you'll love, share and never forget.
And it's only **ten** words!

BUT before we begin, listen up . . .

Apparently, grown-ups get a bit grumpy if you are too excited at bedtime. So, if you're listening to this story, please say out loud . . .

I PROMISE TO GO TO SLEEP AT THE END OF THIS BOOK.

And it's only fair if the grown-up reading
this story makes a promise too ...

I PROMISE TO READ
IN MY BEST
READING VOICE.

Perfect!

Let's get started.

First, you need to do a very serious
voice warm-up...

Ma, ma, ma, Me

Marrrrr PlO

La, La, Looloolooo

la, La,

chicken

Fa, fa, fa, fa, Foo, foo, foo, noodle

Smelly

zzzzzZZZZZZz

Socks

and

Next, have a big stretch, and don't forget to yawn.

Finished? Great!

Make sure you're really comfy.
Plump up all the pillows...

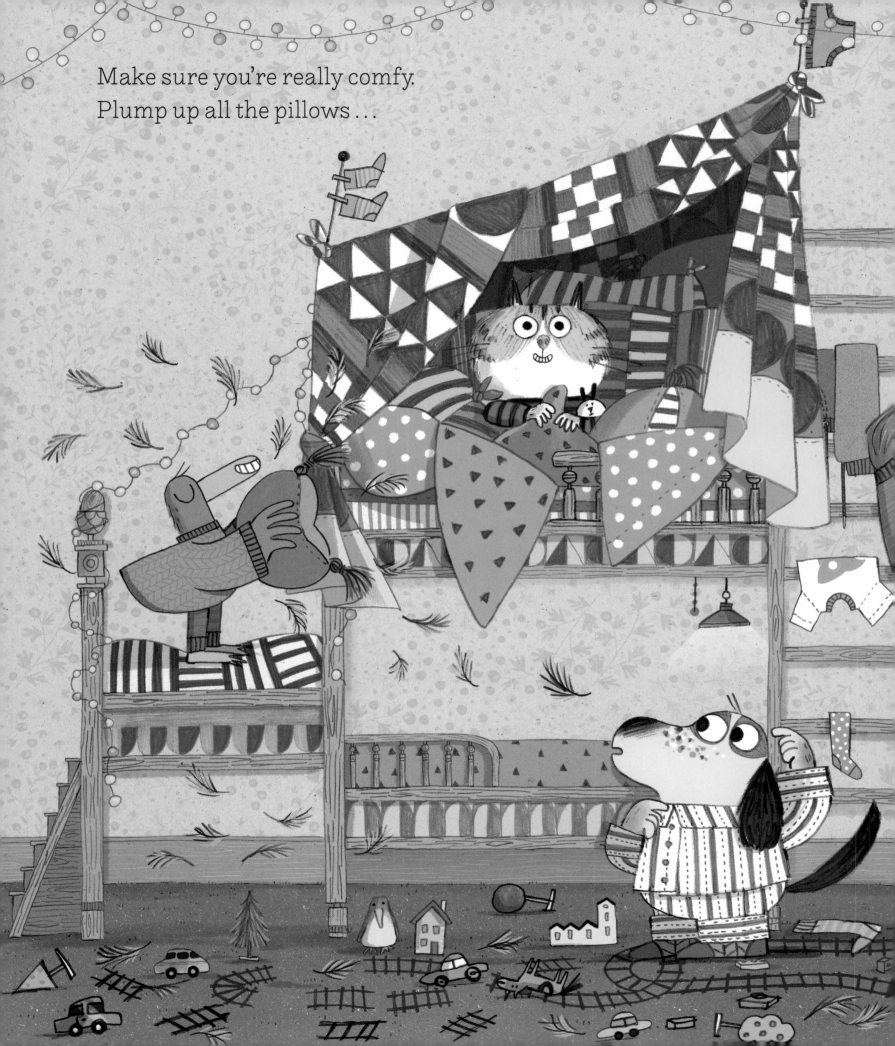

AND any wobbly tummies.

Well done!
Now, where were we?

Oh yes.

A quick instruction
before we carry on...

It's probably a mistake, but sometimes your grown-up
accidentally leaves out a page (or two).
So, do watch them carefully!
You wouldn't want to miss anything, would you?

In fact, why don't you show them how it's done properly?
You'll need to put on a VERY serious face ...
Page-turning is VERY important at bedtime,
I'll have you know.

Get ready.

Wow!

That's a truly marvellous face.
Now — turn the page
(very seriously, remember).

Nice work!

May I continue?

Good.

Once upon a . . .

Oh, hang on.
WAIT!

Have you made sure all
your toys are tucked in?
They'll want to share the
bedtime story too.

You can put them in order
of tallest to smallest, or
in colours and patterns,
OR you could even try
your own ideas?

Off you go.

ZZZZZ

All done?

Check everyone's included.
Don't forget to look . . .

under your blanket (they're not
hiding down there, are they?) . . .

in between your toes ...
under everyone's armpits
(be careful not to tickle them) ...
and, last but NOT least,
up any nose holes (watch out for bogies!).

ZZZZZZZZZ

Fantastic
checking!

Let's do this.

Once upon a . . .

HOLD IT!
I can't believe I nearly missed this out!

Your bedtime story must have a gentle fanfare!

So —
rat-a-tap-tap your imaginary drum,
ting-a-ling-a-ling your triangle,
jiggle-wiggle-shake your tambourine
and, of course, don't forget to give a
teeny-tiny toot on your trumpet.

Amazing!

Here we go.

Once upon a . . .

STOP.
Freeze right there!
I nearly forgot one last thing . . .

You must answer these very important
questions with a tick of your magic finger.

Is everyone here?
Are you all comfy?
Is everyone snuggled up?

Wonderful!

It looks like we're
finally ready for our
ten-word bedtime
story ...

Once upon a bed,
you laughed
and played
and read.

There.
Isn't that the **most brilliant** (quickest) bedtime story ever?

Now, remember you **promised** to go to sleep?

But ... since we're still here,
how about ONE LAST story?

After all, it's only ten words.

Night, night, sleep tight,
dream big, dream bright . . .

the end.

(Until
tomorrow!)